THE LEGEND OF BLUE NINJA - THE ENDER KNIGHTS

AN UNOFFICIAL MINECRAFT BOOK

NILUV RATHI

Contents

Preface

Niluv is a 13 year old currently studying in Grade 10. He is a songwriter, author, gamer and diehard minecraft fan. He was inspired by several minecraft series such as The Legend of Dave the Villager, Diary of a Surfer Villager, and many official Mojang books.

Acknowledgements

I would like to thank my mother, Vinita Rathi and my father, Nilesh Rathi, who encouraged me and helped me to write this book.

Mob Chart

Creeper: A mob that explodes when in range of an enemy. The majority of their species was destroyed by Herobrine's army.

Skeleton: A mob that is armed with a bow, while some of their kind are trained with melee weapons. Spawns in the overworld, and predominantly under the rule of the Necrolord.

Super Skeleton: A genetically mutated skeleton that is significantly stronger than a standard skeleton in every aspect.

Zombie: A mob that engages its enemy in melee combat. Predominantly under the rule of the Necrolord.

Mutant Zombie: A mutated zombie that is approximately five times better in every aspect except strategy and thinking as compared to a zombie.

Zombie Pigman: A mob that lives in the Nether and is trained in either melee combat or with a crossbow. Under the rule of the Pigman King.

Pillager: Mercenaries that exist solely to cause destruction and death. They look like genetically mutated villagers due to their grey skin.

Wither Skeleton: A species of powerful skeletons that are coal in colour and live in the Nether. They can be trained in any form of combat and give the Wither Effect to anyone they engage in melee combat. Under the rule of the Wither Queen.

Spider: Mobs that can cross any terrain or platform, and can web and bite their enemies. Under the rule of Queen Arachnid.

Ghast: A mob that looks sort of like a marshmallow with tentacles. They fly around in the Nether making creepy noises and engage their enemies with heavy fireballs.

Enderman: A mob that teleports and can be trained in any form of combat, and deals very heavy damage when engaged. They serve under the rule of the Endermasters, and the EnderLord.

Vindicator: A more powerful form of pillager. They are usually trained with an axe, and deal very heavy damage when engaged.

Vindicator: The most powerful form of pillager. They

are trained in dark magic, and cast spells to release Chompers and Vexes.

Ravager: A massive beast which pillagers ride and use to destroy obstructions and obliterate enemies.

The Story So Far

Three teenage Super-Soldiers, Neel, Ron, and Adam were three regular teenagers before the war. Then, one day, Herobrine's monstrous army arrived and destroyed everything. Adam met Neel and Ron in the ghost city of Biggerton, and they joined a resistance group known as Fort Torro.

Herobrine and the tyrannical Queen of the Wither Skeletons created a terrifying, mutated version known as the Wither Storm. The resistance uncovered the missing piece of the puzzle, that the two villains had created the Wither Storm with the help of the Command Block, which was supposedly the most powerful block in Minecraft.

The Wither Storm attacked Fort Torro and was successful in destroying it. It left no trace of the once prosperous haven. The surviving residents of Fort Torro met with another resistance group known as Fort Linux, and the two groups banded together as one and built the Iron Fortress. The Iron Fortress was heavily damaged in the Second Battle of the Either Storm, but they claimed victory by defeating the Wither Storm and destroying the Command Block.

General SlickArrow betrayed Herobrine and looted the treasury. He escaped the palace and joined the resistance. He now fights with the Ender Forces.

Two wither skeletons discovered their Queen's treacherous nature and decided to betray their allegiance to her. They were the first to discover the Wither Storm and were rescued by General Webley and his Ender Soldiers.

A rebel group formed in the centre of Herobrine's palace itself, led by Zvet and Quane, a zombie and skeleton respectively. They recruited several members and were behind the destruction of the original Command Block. Herobrine sensed the presence of an insurgency but is still yet to uncover the people behind it.

The legend continues...

Prologue

Herobrine paced inside the golden walls of his throne room, the shiny golden floor and walls vibrating with his every step. For a brief moment, he remembered the good old days when he pillaged rich towns and cities with his monstrous army before there weren't any cities and towns left for him to conquer.

But his troubles came back to him when an iron-clad zombie came rushing into the throne room, heavily wounded.

"My Lord, we are under attack! The Seventh Zombie Division has been destroyed! Please help' The zombie was cut off when an arrow struck the exposed part of his neck, and he poofed.

Herobrine shook his head distastefully and sent his elite guards to deal with the threat. He was far too busy to deal with rebels. He just lost his biggest wild card, the Command Block, permanently. He had the idea of contacting an old ally of his, the NecroLord, but he had no clue where to find him. The NecroLord had been seemingly gone for the last few decades, and there had been no sign of his presence in all the realms of Minecraftia.

Before his disappearance, he had given the undead

monsters underneath him the command to serve
Herobrine. This aided the white-eyed glitch heavily,
but the two never met after that.

So until he found a way to reach the NecroLord,
Herobrine would just have to figure out something
else.

CHAPTER ONE

EXP LEVEL

The Iron Fortress was busy conducting repairs after the battle with the Wither Storm. Several parts of the walls had been destroyed, and the East Wall had been completely vaporised. The only remains of the East Wall were the obsidian foundation at surface level.

"I don't remember this happening," said Ron, scratching his head.

"Probably because you were at a different wall," Neel reminded him.

"Hold on, if this wall is gone, does that mean all the Trebuchets were destroyed as well?" asked Adam, his eyes wide.

"Unfortunately, yes," said Captain Flerra, who was passing by with a book and quill in her hand, observing the damages done to the Iron Fortress.

Neel looked around at the destruction with disdain. "We could have prevented this if we were stronger..."

"I agree. We simply had too many casualties in this battle, and this is just not acceptable for super soldiers," said Adam, shaking his head with regret, remembering the precious hours he had wasted messing around with his smithing table during the afternoon every day.

"Then let's train and beat their butts!" Ron chimed in, a somewhat serious look on his face.

The three stepped beyond the walls, into the unchanging plains that stretched around the Iron Fortress. They could see a dark oak forest in the distance, and Ron could make out the silhouettes of mobs roaming the shadowy grounds of the forest. The three got out their signature weapons and readied themselves for a fight. Ron simply stood there, his sniper resting at his side, knowing that a single shot from his rifle would be lethal if he joined the fight.

Adam opened his mouth to say something, but his eyes widened in surprise and no words came out of his mouth as Neel lunged at him with his blades out in front of him. He barely raised his longsword in time to block the attack, but Neel did not hesitate in going for the offence again. He followed in with a thrust when the blade seemingly flew out of his hand with a sharp clang.

"Are you guys crazy? You'll kill each other with your real weapons! Ron, you didn't think you should stop them?" scolded Flerra, who came running over with a suppressed pistol.

"Sodium Hydride, bro," said Ron, shrugging.

"What?" asked Flerra, baffled.

"Nah," grinned Ron, proud of his joke.

Flerra facepalmed. "Idiot... alright, there's a wooden shed in the far corner of the training grounds from the entrance. There should be wooden replicas of your weapons in there, so I don't want to see you being reckless again."

They followed Captain Flerra's orders, retrieved wooden replicas of their iconic weapons from the designated shed, and returned to the plains.

"Okay, guys. Let's do this!" said Neel, enthusiastically executing the same lunge he had carried out before, expecting the same results.

This time Adam was well prepared for this and effortlessly blocked the attack. The clangs of their blades clashing against one another echoed through the plains. Adam decided to confuse Neel by crouching low and sweeping the ground with his longsword.

Meanwhile, Ron was wondering what would happen if he fired his wooden sniper rifle. For one thing, he was still bewildered at the fact that such a contraption could exist. It disobeyed the very laws of physics! Then again, there were floating trees, so that wasn't a really good argument.

Ron decided to stop thinking about it and just pulled on the trigger.

Smack!

Neel was stopped in his tracks just as he was about to strike Adam in the head.

"What in the Nether was that?!" exclaimed Neel, rubbing his chest where the projectile had struck him.

The gun appeared to be able to fire wooden bullets, roughly the same size as a regular bullet. But, the bullets were blunt-ended and blocky, unlike regular bullets that were lethal. Ron grinned. This was going to be fun.

Since he couldn't morph his gun like his real sniper, he decided to just use it old-fashioned style. He couldn't just spam fire because the reload time and recoil of the gun were much more than his mysterious rifle, so he just aimed and shot anyone who got close to him. Neel and Adam weren't able to get over a ten-block radius of Ron, as he kept driving them back with the force of his bullets. That was until his gun didn't fire when he pulled the trigger.

"Looks like you're out of ammo. What are you gonna do now?" said Neel, a sly grin creeping onto his face.

He seized the opportunity and rushed towards Ron, his blades raised above his head. Adam realised what was going to happen and threw his longsword at Neel with pinpoint accuracy. Neel managed to strike Ron down, knocking him out, but the airborne longsword slammed into his head, shoving him into the dirt. He did not get back up, so he was probably knocked unconscious.

"I win!" cheered Adam.

He then heard a strange chime coming from the direction of his inventory. He opened his inventory in pursuit of the sound but found nothing.

"That was your EXP bar," said Flerra, who was walking towards her cabin.

"My what-now?" replied Adam, confused.

Flerra stopped in her tracks and looked at Adam with an annoyed look on her face.

"What? What's an EXP bar?" asked Adam, shrugging.

Flerra sighed. "EXP means experience points. Do you know what enchanting is?"

Adam nodded.

Flerra continued. "You use experience points to enchant. When you enchant something, your experience points disappear and are consumed in the process. It's like lapis lazuli, it has no other use, but that use alone is important enough. Do you follow?"
"Yeah, okay, but how do you get experience points? By training and sparring?" said Adam.

"A variety of activities. Training, farming, breeding, smelting, and all the other mundane things. The most powerful enchants require an experience level of thirty. That's over a thousand experience points. What's your experience level?" asked Flerra.

"How do I check?" asked Adam, rummaging through his inventory once more.

Flerra face-palmed. "It's not in your inventory. Do you see the green bar just above your hot bar? That's your EXP bar. What does it say?"

"Thirty. No, that can't be right. You said that's over a thousand experience points. But it says thirty," said Adam, scratching his head.

Flerra's jaw dropped. "How is that even possible? It's unheard of for a child of your age to have an experience level of over twenty! What have you even been doing lately?"

"I don't know. I love to mess around with my furnace and smithing table," said Adam. "You said smelting things gives you experience points."

"It's a remarkable achievement, you should be proud of yourself," smiled Flerra. "What do you say we enchant that greatsword of yours?"

Adam grinned at the prospect of getting an edge over his friends. "You've got yourself a deal!"

CHAPTER TWO

Goofing Around

After Flerra had briefed Adam on the basics of enchanting, the two went their separate ways again. Adam dragged his friends back to their underground apartment, while Flerra resumed her duties.

Once Neel and Ron were awake, Adam relayed what Flerra had told him.

"Whoa, so now you can enchant your sword? That's not fair! Why am I not level thirty?" complained Ron, looking down at his EXP bar. "I'm only level nineteen!"

"Maybe sleeping all day while I was being productive wasn't such a good idea, huh?" snorted Adam.

Ron narrowed his eyes. "I'll get there soon enough, you'll see."

Neel broke in. "What enchantment are you planning on getting?"

"Knockback?" suggested Adam.

"What about the fire aspect?" said Ron, with a gleam of mischief in his eyes.

"Nope, nah, not happening. You're probably gonna steal my sword and set fire to every building in a thousand-block radius!" exclaimed Adam.

Ron grinned and Neel laughed.

"When are you going to get the enchantment though?" asked Neel.

"Do we have anything to do now?" replied Adam.

"Let's go!" said Neel.

In response, Ron lazily fell face-flat on the carpet.

"Alright, fine, maybe in a couple of hours," said Adam.

Neel shrugged and went through a doorway into his compact bedroom. The three of them each had a small bedroom to themselves, where they were free to do whatever they wanted. All three rooms could be entered only through the medium-sized living room, where they had two sofas and a few armchairs all surrounding a fireplace and a cosy mini-library. Another doorway led to the kitchen which was decent-sized and had an island in the middle that served as the dining table.

Ron got up from the carpet, grinning. He stretched his arms and went into his room, and started snoring, much to Adam's annoyance. Sighing, Adam shrugged and took out an old book from the mini-library, and plopped down on his armchair with a smile.

Neel walked out of his room a few minutes later.

"I'm bored," he yawned.

"About time," grinned Adam. "Let's go wake up Ron."

Once Ron was awake, Adam grabbed his greatsword and the three walked out of their underground apartment, Ron complaining about how he was woken out of an awesome dream.

They headed straight for Flerra's oak wooden cabin, which looked almost identical to the one that used to be in Fort Torro. Ron peeked through one of the glass windows and saw Flerra reading a piece of paper and muttering something with an angry expression.

Ron turned to his friends and made a weird sign with his hand.

Adam scrunched his face up and began walking towards the door.

Ron's eyes widened as Adam knocked on the door, still looking at Ron as if he was having a seizure.

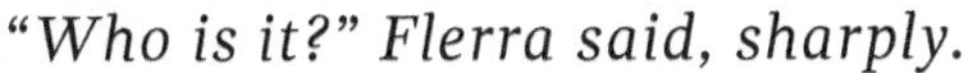

"Who is it?" Flerra said, sharply.

Adam opened the door and peeked inside. Flerra's expression relaxed and she beckoned them to come inside.

"I assume you boys have come to get Adam's enchantment," said Flerra, setting her papers down with a sigh.

"Yeah. But what's that you got so mad about?" blurted Ron.

Neel glared at Ron and Adam shook his head.

"It's none of our busi-," Neel was cut off as Flerra raised her hand.

Flerra ra "Have you kids heard of the rebellion in Herobrine's palace?"

They shook their heads.

"Well, three of their members were cut down in a recent fight, and the others are in hiding. One of their dead was their skeleton leader."

"Whoa. That's... unfortunate. Are they going to come to the Iron Fortress?" asked Neel.

"No, they will keep their cover and try to remain low before the incident blows over."

As the conversation was going on, a sparkling obsidian-diamond table caught Adam's eye. He walked over to the table and opened the book which floated above it.

"It says I can't enchant yet, I need to be level fifty," said Adam.

"That's weird. A regular max-level enchant only requires level thirty. How is that possible?" Flerra scratched her head.

"Maybe it's because we're super soldiers," shrugged Neel.

CHAPTER THREE

WHERE ARE THE KNIGHTS?

"*The Wither Skeletons are causing us a lot of trouble these days. Just recently we lost one of our precious elite squadrons," said Scintherus*

"*That is unfortunate. How many elite squadrons do we have remaining?" asked Conlivius*

"*We used to have ten squads, but now we only have nine," stated Scintherus.*

"*What do you suggest we do?" asked another Endermaster, Verithius.*

"*I'm not sure, to be honest," replied Scintherus.*

"Say, what happened to the EnderLord and his Ender Knights?" asked the fourth Endermaster, Drosirius.

There were four Endermasters in the Ender Council. Scintherus, the War Master, Conlivius, the Resource Master, Verithius, the Civilian Master, and Drosirius, the Research Master.

Each Endermaster had a big role to play in the management of the End. If even one of them failed to complete their responsibility, the End would fall into chaos. Well, everyone except Drosirius. He was the research master, so he just upgraded the efficiency of everything and designed new machinery and all of that tech-y stuff.

"Ah, yes. The Ender Knights. The EnderLord told us almost half a year ago he would be sending the legendary Ender Knights to help us defeat the Wither Skeletons. We should summon him and ask him what happened to that thought." declared Scintherus.

The Council all agreed to Scintherus' suggestion, and they called the summoner to start the ritual. That was the only way they could summon the EnderLord.

The ritual consisted of the summoner chanting some weird commands and some chorus fruit and redstone dust strewn across the floor in a hexagonal shape. Even the Endermasters thought that the EnderLord had gone overboard with this one, but they couldn't question it.

After a few minutes, the EnderLord suddenly appeared on his summoning pad. The Endermasters and the summoner got down from their thrones and kneeled down to the EnderLord.

"At ease, endermen. For what reason have you summoned me today?" asked the EnderLord.

"We were wondering what happened to your sending of the Ender Knights," Scintherus responded, rising from his position.

"Ah, yes. I completely forgot about that. In your next battle, the Ender Knights will assist you." The EnderLord declared.

"*Thank you, my lord.*"

The EnderLord decided to go now. He simply vanished, leaving the Endermasters shaking their heads.

"*I doubt he will remember this time,*" *said Conlivius.*

"*Do not doubt the Lord. He will keep his promise,*" *said Scintherus, angrily.*

There was suddenly a massive explosion out of the Ender Fortress. The ground shook, and a couple of end stone blocks fell out of the roof.

"*We are under attack! I repeat, WE ARE UNDER ATTACK!*" *The alarm buzzed and started shining red.*

All the Endermasters except for Scintherus headed down to the emergency bunker.

"They are all cowards. They wouldn't even fight if their lives depended on it." Scintherus shook his head.

He activated his energy blade and teleported outside.

CHAPTER FOUR

ARRIVAL

Everyone knew what was attacking the Endermen. It was the wither skeletons, obviously. Nobody knew how the Wither Kingdom could spare these many soldiers. The army looked like it had over a thousand soldiers in it, around a hundred ghasts, and a few withers. A formidable army.

"Sir Scintherus!" yelled a voice.

It was General Webley. It had been a long time since the two had last met since Webley was tasked with assisting the Iron Fortress.

"Webley! Good to see you! Let's end these fools!" Scintherus pumped his fist.

Webley saluted and teleported into battle, SlickArrow, Gabriel and Trey in pursuit.

Scintherus teleported onto the wall where he surveyed the scene. The endermen had the upper hand for now, but Scintherus didn't think that would last for long. Once the ghasts were in range of fire, the endermen would be pelted with fireballs back-to-back.

He exchanged his energy blade for an energy bow and started shooting arrows into the oncoming army. Several of them hit their targets, but a few missed and hit the end stone. The wither skeletons were wearing either full gold or full netherite armour, so most of them barely even flinched as the arrows deflected off of their armour.

"This won't do. This definitely won't do," thought Scintherus, frantically. "Where are those Ender Knights? Now would be a good time, EnderLord!"

As if on cue, a roar echoed throughout the battlefield. It was the roar of an Ender Dragon. There were several of them, approaching the wither skeleton army from all sides. About ten of them in total, with endermen riding them, clad head to toe in some strange armour. They spat purple fire across the army, burning and poofing many skeletons. A few even got off their dragons to fight the wither skeletons themselves, their strange swords melting straight through the armour of the wither skeletons.

Many of the archers on the walls stopped firing arrows to marvel at the Ender Knights. This gave the wither skeletons at the front line an advantage over the endermen, and endermen rapidly started poofing.

"Archers, stop staring and continue your fire!" yelled Scintherus.

The archers shook out of their trance and started raining arrows on the wither skeletons.

It was clear to the wither skeletons that they couldn't win this battle. The Ender Knights were too powerful. But, they couldn't retreat anymore because a couple of Ender Knights destroyed the withers and the nether portal. Many of them continued fighting, while others tried to surrender. In the end, only one wither skeleton survived, who surrendered and was thrown into the interrogation chamber. Many tried to surrender, but their superiors cut them down for treason.

The Ender Knights grouped up and approached Scintherus.

"Sir Scintherus. The Ender Knights at your service," the Ender Knight leader bowed. The other Ender Knights followed and bowed as well.

"At ease, Knights. You have arrived at a crucial time. The Wither Skeletons keep launching attacks like this one, and after this, they will most likely send an even larger one. I want all of you to patrol the End. Alert me as soon as you see any signs of the Wither Skeletons."

The Ender Knights saluted and got on their dragons. They waved goodbye to the other ender soldiers and flew away to patrol the End.

CHAPTER FIVE

PLANNING

Scintherus was confident that the endermen would triumph over the wither skeletons. With the Ender Knights patrolling the End, there was no way the Wither Queen could launch a surprise attack. This way, Scintherus could easily focus on training more elite ender soldiers and creating a massive army to destroy the Wither Kingdom. Once the Wither Kingdom was destroyed, they would have almost complete control over the Nether, as the Wither Kingdom was the most powerful settlement. The Ghast Kingdom could be easily overcome, and the Pigman kingdom was small fry. As for the blazes and the magma cubes, the magma cubes were neutral in the war and the blazes were enslaved by the Wither Skeletons.

"Webley, how many elite soldiers do we have in total?" Scintherus asked, starting preparations for the army.

"Around sixty, sir. Most of them were killed in the Wither Skeleton attacks, and many were killed in the Second Battle of the Wither Storm.

"What? This won't do. We must train more. How many normal soldiers do we have?"

Webley winced. "Not nearly as many as we had before the beginning of these attacks. Our numbers have been reduced to around two thousand."

Scintherus shook his head, concerned about how they were going to fare about this.

"We must train more soldiers. The wither skeletons attack us with raiding parties almost the size of our army! With this small amount of troops, there is no way we can conquer the Nether. Hire more trainers. Build more training grounds. Craft more weapons. Do whatever you have to do to increase our numbers. The Wither Kingdom has to be destroyed." Scintherus ordered.

General Webley saluted in response and teleported away. Scintherus headed back to the Ender Council to tell them about the situation. He teleported to the entrance of the castle and then walked inside.

"Scintherus! Has the attack been dealt with?" Verithius called out.

"Indeed, Verithius. With the assistance of the Ender Knights, we easily destroyed the oncoming army." Scintherus responded.

"Great. I assume you have come back from your work to speak to me and Conlivius about something other than this?"

"I would like to call another meeting of the council. This is something we all need to talk about."

"It shall be done."

Verithius sent one of his servants to call Drosirius from his lab. After a few minutes, all four of the Endermasters were gathered in the main room.

"*What is this matter of urgency? I was designing an upgraded energy bow,*" said Drosirius, annoyed.

"*I have called this meeting to discuss the state of our army. It seems that-*'' started Scintherus.

"*I thought managing the army was your responsibility,*" sneered Drosirius.

"*Drosirius, do not interrupt Scintherus. He may want something from us. Be quiet, or leave,*" scolded Conlivius.

Drosirius glared at Conlivius but said nothing.

"*Continue,*" gestured Conlivius.

Scintherus sighed. "As I was saying, before I was rudely interrupted," He looked at Drosirius, who rolled his eyes. "*It seems that our army is at an all-time low. We only have around sixty elite soldiers and about two thousand ender soldiers. We have had heavy casualties in our recent battles.”*

Scintherus looked towards Conlivius. “I need you to triple your supply of resources to our military. I know it sounds a bit much, but we need to take matters into our own hands and defeat the Wither Kingdom before they try anything else against us.”

Conlivius studied Scintherus for a few moments then nodded.

“Drosirius, I need you to work on better weapons for our troops, and better fighting techniques if you can too. Verithius, please recruit as many soldiers as you can. The more numbers, the better,” said Scintherus.

The Endermasters all agreed and then went about their ways.

"Wait, Scintherus, before you go, are you sure it is wise to attack the Wither Kingdom head-on?" questioned Conlivius.

"It is too late to think about that. If we wait any longer than we need to, there is a chance the Wither Queen will come up with another super weapon or something. We need to end this now!" replied Scintherus.

"I agree with you, but we will sustain too many casualties. Perhaps while the Ender soldiers are training, we can figure out a plan to somehow destroy the Wither Kingdom without losing too many men ourselves," said Conlivius.

"I will call all the Ender Generals and see what we can do. Thank you for the advice, Conlivius."

"Anytime, brother."

Scintherus walked towards the War Council room and found one of his servants standing outside the entrance.

"Carter, please call my generals and tell them all to urgently meet me in the War Council room," Scintherus told the servant.

"As you wish, sir."

Carter walked out of the castle and then teleported away. Scintherus walked into the War Council room and looked towards the bookshelves.

"Maybe I can check that book I found the other day, 'Laying Siege to a Kingdom'." He thought aloud.

He walked over to the bookshelves and started searching for the book.

"Sir Scintherus, you called for us?" came a voice behind him.

Scintherus spun around and saw his four generals at the door.

"General Webley, General Crushmore, General Kinterro and General Berserker. Come in," gestured Scintherus.

The four generals came in and sat on some chairs. Scintherus did the same, taking in a deep breath.

"As I have already informed General Webley, we are going to be laying siege to the Wither Kingdom. I aim to take it down once and for all and kill the Wither Queen and if possible, even the WitherLord. Do you all follow?" explained Scintherus.

"Yes, sir," said the generals, in unison.

"General Kinterro, I want you to assist Fort Torro instead of General Webley in whatever task they are doing. General Crushmore, I want you and General Berserker to coordinate with the other Endermasters and enlarge our army. General Webley, you and I will go to the Nether and we will infiltrate and destroy the

Ghast Kingdom from within," announced Scintherus, determined.

The Generals saluted and went on their way, except for Webley, who stayed back to talk with Scintherus.

"Sir, why the Ghast Kingdom? Why not any other kingdom such as the Pigman Kingdom?" asked Webley.

"The Pigman Kingdom is already at war with the new renegade Piglins. The Piglins are trying to overthrow the Pigman King and many rebellions have started to form within the kingdom itself. We have no war with the magma cubes and the blazes will take any opportunity to destroy the Wither Kingdom themselves. The Ghast Kingdom is the next step in ensuring our victory over the Wither Kingdom," declared Scintherus.

Webley nodded and went deep into thought.

PIGLIN UPRISING

"Fire! Kill them all! Don't spare anyone!"

Explosions echoed throughout the Nether, bodies strewn across the netherrack. Fires raged, and lava dropped from the sky. Hell was breaking loose.

"Die, piglin scum!"

Zombie pigmen soldiers slashed at Piglins left and right, and archers fired arrow after arrow, cannon after cannon. Piglins and pigmen alike poofed left and right, lifeless bodies falling to the ground.

"Don't leave any-" The Zombie Pigman commander was cut short as the Piglin leader charged through the iron door behind him and kicked him off the edge of the wall.

The commander fell past the netherrack cliff straight into the lava below, screaming all the way.

"Surrender, zombie pigmen! We have no wish to fight you any longer!" yelled the piglin leader.

Some of the zombie pigmen raised their hands, surrendering, but many charged the commander. Of course, the other piglins made short work of the remaining pigmen.

The commander smiled, his plan finally coming to fruition. The piglins had started spawning in the Nether around the same time as Netherite was discovered and the new biomes of the Nether had started appearing. The piglins had tried to make *peace with the pigmen at first, but the pigmen slaughtered them, calling them inferior and trying to enslave them. The piglins realised that the pigmen would not negotiate, so the leader decided that the piglins would keep to themselves, and act when the time was right.*

The zombie pigmen had forgotten about them after their first encounter, giving the piglins the element of surprise. When the zombie pigmen had their guard down, supplying most of their resources to the Wither Kingdom to fund their war against the End, the piglins decided to strike. They had captured many of the Blackstone bastions and outposts of the zombie pigmen, and the entire Pigman Kingdom was coming to an end.

"Lord Boarshead, what are your commands?" asked a piglin brute.

Piglin brutes were a stronger breed of piglins, using golden axes instead of golden swords and crossbows. They were the elite force of the piglin army.

"*Tell the zombie pigmen that they are welcome to join our army, or they can go south to the civilian area of our land. Any attempt to go back to the zombie pigmen army will not be tolerated,*" said Lord Boarshead.

The piglin brute saluted and jumped off the edge of the bastion, easily landing on the edge of the cliff below.

Lord Boarshead sat down on a Blackstone chair. He knew the hard part of erasing the Pigman King's tyranny was coming. Taking out the outposts and forts was the easy part since most of the Pigman Army was concentrated at the capital, Pigtopia City.

His original plan was to capture the outposts and bastions one by one then easily overcome the army at Pigtopia City, but looking at the sheer numbers at even the bastions, he knew he would have to think about this strategically. If they rushed at the Pigman King's army blindly, the piglins would suffer heavy casualties.

While Lord Boarshead was deep in thought, a zombie pigman snuck up behind him. No one noticed the pigman, as they thought that he was now passive. He was just about to cut off Lord Boarshead's head with his golden sword when a piglin brute's enchanted golden axe embedded itself in his back, sending him sprawling on the ground.

"What happened?" asked Lord Boarshead, in shock.

"Renegade pigman tried to kill you." grunted the brute.

Lord Boarshead nodded his thanks at the brute and told the rest of the elites to stay alert. It would seem that some pigmen were loyal enough to the Pigman King to the point they would lay down their lives for him even when all hope was lost. The piglins had to stay alert and act fast.

Lord Boarshead did not want to annihilate the zombie pigman race, contrasting with what the Pigman King wanted to do. He was willing to have peace with them, and even righteously allowed the pigmen to live amongst the piglins in peace. But looking at the situation, the pigmen could betray them and kill the troops at any time.

Lord Boarshead would have to remove all the zombie pigmen from the army until the Pigman King was removed from power. The piglins could not risk the pigmen getting any information from any renegades or traitors.

CHAPTER SEVEN

CORRUPTED

Scintherus was relaxing in his room, thinking about how he and General Webley were going to infiltrate the Ghast Kingdom. He had assumed he would have peace, since the Ender Knights were patrolling and protecting the End.

Alas, so was not to happen.

"WE ARE UNDER ATTACK! I REPEAT, WE ARE UNDER ATTACK!" blared the alarm.

Scintherus choked on the air and sat up straight.

"What in the Nether?!"

He equipped his energy machete and teleported outside. He looked around, seeing many soldiers running around frantically, trying to find their weapons and get outside, and also wondering what in Minecraft was going on.

"Sir Scintherus! Sir Scintherus!" called a voice.

It was General Webley. Scintherus teleported over to him and asked what was going on.

"It seems that the Ender Knights did not alert us about this attack. There is a massive army on the horizon, bigger than any army that has come to attack us before. We may have to evacuate, due to our low numbers," explained Webley.

"Why did the Ender Knights not tell us about this? But, that is something we will wonder about another time. Right now, we must focus on the task at hand."

Scintherus and Webley teleported onto the walls and surveyed the area. There were, as Webley said, thousands of wither skeletons charging into the End. It was as if the Wither Queen had sent her whole army.

"This doesn't feel right. Why would the Wither Queen send an army to capture the End if she knew that the Ender Knights were guarding us now?" said Scintherus, shaking his head.

"Sir Scintherus! We must retreat! We are suffering heavy losses!" said General Crushmore, teleporting onto the wall.

"Where is General Berserker?" asked Scintherus.

"He is over there above the gate, coordinating our archers," he pointed.

Scintherus realised that the army was too big for the End to handle.

"Give the order to retreat! We shall go through the portal to The Iron Fortress!"

General Crushmore teleported away. Scintherus saw the army of the End gradually retreating through the gate, the archers covering them. He realised that Webley must have been with the ground troops, and saw him injured inside the castle.

"Webley! Are you alright?" asked Scintherus, frantically.

"I'll live. Go, handle the others!" said Webley.

Scintherus teleported inside the castle and saw several injured troops being escorted into the portal. The Endermasters were helping out with the escorting, as several explosions echoed throughout the fortress.

It was then that the endermen heard the roar of an Ender Dragon.

"We have been saved! It is the Ender Knights!" cheered a soldier.

An Ender Dragon flew through the archway and into the fortress near the portal. The Knight atop the dragon seemed to be out of breath and scared.

"It is I, Sirius, leader of the Ender Knights. My fellow knights have seemingly betrayed us. They are working with the Wither Queen and I have concluded that they had been corrupted by her. I am the only one who has remained incorrupt," explained the Knight.

The Knight coughed a few times and lost a few hearts.

45

"I- I have the same effect. I will be corrupted in a few days if I am not cured before then," coughed the Knight.

It was at that moment that the Ender Lord chose to show up.

"Fat lot of help you've been!" yelled Drosirius.

"I apologise, Drosirius, I had no idea of these recent happenings. Scintherus, your call was correct. We must retreat. As for the remaining Ender Knight, I'm not entirely sure what the cure for this effect is," said the Ender Lord.

THE END IS LOST

The Iron Fortress was still completing the final repairs on the walls when the ender soldiers started coming out of the End Portal. Ron and Neel were close to upgrading to the first tier.

Captain Flerra had no clue of the happenings in the End, as none of the generals had visited the Iron Fortress after the battle with the Wither Storm. That was until General Kinterro had arrived in the Iron Fortress.

"You say Scintherus is planning to siege the Wither Kingdom?" said Captain Flerra.

"That is correct," replied General Kinterro.

"*Does he require any assi-*" *Flerra was cut off.*

Scintherus suddenly teleported inside the room. He had a massive wound on his shoulder that was bandaged up.

"*We've lost... the End...*" *said Scintherus, out of breath.*

"*What happened?!*" *exclaimed Flerra, her eyes looking back and forth at Scintherus' would and his face.*

"*I assume Kinterro has already told you about the arrival of the Ender Knights,*" *said Scintherus.*

Flerra nodded.

Scintherus continued. "*It turns out they were recently corrupted and went under the control of the Wither Queen. A massive army of wither skeletons, tens of thousands of them, along with the corrupted knights took over the End. We lost many soldiers, so we decided to retreat. General Webley is also heavily injured and he is resting in the infirmary. The only Knight who is still with us is their leader."*

Flerra was shocked, as was General Kinterro.

"Sir Scintherus, what shall we do?" asked General Kinterro.

"There is only one thing left to do," said Scintherus, grimly. "We are probably the next target. Due to recent happenings, I assume Herobrine will strike the Fortress next. We must prepare for a siege."

Flerra and Kinterro both nodded, and Kinterro went outside.

"Scintherus, is that the Ender Lord?" asked Flerra, staring at the giant enderman outside her window.

"Yes. He arrived just as we were about to escape the End. It seems that he is finally joining the war himself," nodded Scintherus.

The giant enderman suddenly disappeared, and Flerra blinked in surprise. He reappeared in the cabin, having to stoop to avoid banging his head on the roof.

"Greetings, Flerra. I am the Ender Lord," said the Ender Lord.

Flerra and Scintherus both bowed, showing respect.

The Ender Lord turned to Scintherus. "Scintherus, I have a plan. I will personally train fifteen new Ender Knights to combat the corrupted Knights. I require your best elite soldiers for this quest."

"I need my best warriors on the battlefield, yet you want me to send them away. Will they return in time to be of use? Or am I simply offering them as sacrifices to a battle they cannot win?"

At this moment, someone barged through the door.

"Yo Captain, Adam just hit level fifty!" Ron pumped his fist.

Neel and Adam were outside the door, shaking their heads.

Flerra slapped her head. *"Ron, I'm in the middle of something here."*

Scintherus and the Ender Lord chuckled. Ron realised what was going on and bowed.

"It's good that Adam is ready for an upgrade. Now, can you give us some privacy?" said

Flerra.

Once the super soldiers were out of hearing, Scintherus looked towards the Ender Lord.

"I shall assign my best elites to you. Flerra, the Ender Lord and I will be departing your presence now. After I command my elites to go with the Ender Lord, I shall help with the preparations of the defences," said Scintherus, before teleporting along with the Ender Lord.

Flerra was angry now. Things were finally starting to go well, and now the allied forces had lost the End. It was now or never. While the endermen prepared for an all-out siege, the Iron Fortress would make the first move.

"After all my planning, after all the strategies I formulated, it still ended like this. What am I going to tell the soldiers, let alone the civilians? How can I ask them to serve beside me when I let their homeland be taken by the Nether?" Scintherus thought, in despair.

CHAPTER NINE

WHAT'S GOING ON?

"Ron, Neel, and Adam? You want me to call the super soldiers?" asked one of Captain Flerra's guards.

"Yes Tom, tell the super soldiers to meet me as soon as possible," said Captain Flerra.

The guard nodded and departed the cabin. A few minutes later, he returned with the super soldiers.

"Captain, you asked for us?" said Neel.

"Yes. I want to send you three on a mission along with Commander Josh. We've lost the End to the wither skeletons, and I want you three to destroy the Spider Queen, Arachnid. Total annihilation, no survivors," *said Captain Flerra.*

"I thought we destroyed the Spider Queen when we first came to Fort Torro? You know, with Sir Scintherus?" said Neel.

"You wounded her. She is much more powerful now, and her Spider Army has been growing exponentially according to our scouts. If we let her take the battle to us, then we will be too weak to stop another attack from the Wither Skeletons. That is why I ask you to destroy the Spider Queen and her army. If you kill the Queen, her spiders will have no figurehead to follow and will be unimportant to us."

"But wasn't she already very powerful last time? We were almost killed and we lost all the trebuchets! Do we even have any more trebuchets?" said Adam.

Flerra sighed. "Come with me. I have something much better than trebuchets."

Flerra pressed a button, and to the shock of the three super soldiers, her desk moved aside and revealed a trapdoor in the flooring. Flerra grinned at the surprised faces of the teens and opened the trapdoor. There was a ladder leading down to a pitch-black room. Flerra went down the ladder, and Neel, Ron and

Adam followed suit.

"Captain Flerra. Who are these children you have brought with you?" asked a gruff voice.

"Devlin, these are the super soldiers. I have brought them here to show them the new weapon."

The voice sounded uncertain. "These children are the super soldiers? These kids are the ones who were so instrumental in the battle with the Wither Storm?"

"What's it to you, mate? You've been living under a rock or something?" sneered Ron.

This was when Devlin decided to come out of the shadows. Devlin was a massive enderman. He had big arms with rippling muscles, an eight-pack, and was probably twice the size of a normal enderman. Ron's face became paler than Neel thought was possible and was practically shaking in his boots.

"Keep quiet, you insolent little brat," spat Devlin.

Devlin sneered at Ron's terrified expression and went back into the shadows. He moved aside so that the group could pass and grinned as Ron quick-walked away from him.

Once they were a safe distance away from Devlin, Ron decided to enquire about him.

"Why was that guy so massive?" asked Ron.

"Devlin is an executioner enderman. Executioner endermen are the strongest natural race of endermen. They are typically top security prison guards as only they can hold most of our prisoners, but since this new technology we have in this secret area is of critical importance, Devlin guards this area," explained Flerra.

"What is this device you speak of anyway?" asked Adam.

"Well, uh, it's a sort of laser rifle which-"

"Laser rifle, cool! What does it do though?" interrupted Ron.

"Will you let me explain? It is a rifle that shoots out three laser beams per magazine that last five seconds each. The laser beam itself is capable of burning through obsidian. Unfortunately, making one of these magazines for the laser rifle is extremely hard, so I doubt the engineers have been able to make many of them," said Flerra.

"Interesting. So, you think that with this laser device, we can burn a hole through the Spider Queen and kill her?" asked Neel.

"In theory, it should work. Unless of course, the Spider Queen's body is tougher than obsidian. In that case, we would be well and truly screwed."

CHAPTER TEN

SECRET WEAPON

The group reached the end of the entrance. They came to a small opening where they saw two more massive executioner endermen.

"Who goes there?" asked one of them.

"These children with me are the super soldiers. I am bringing them inside to show them the device," answered Flerra.

This time the endermen did not question Flerra and simply nodded for them to pass through.

"I thought they were about to make a scene again," said Ron.

They opened the small door and entered a large cavern with several small rooms and tables. The room was a giant mess, with strange substances and papers lying about everywhere. Engineers and scientists were running around, doing whatever it was they were doing.

Flerra led the group towards a large table in the corner, where several engineers were milling about.

After a few seconds, the engineers realised Flerra's presence.

"Captain Flerra! Are you here to check on the laser rifle?" said one of the engineers, a short, plump man with bright red cheeks.

"Yes, Adrian. How many magazines have you guys been able to create?"

Adrian rubbed his chin with his short, stubby fingers. "The magazines are very hard to make, Captain. We only managed to make two magazines in the short time you gave us. If you gave us a bit more time, we could make a few more."

"No, this is very urgent. If we do not complete this mission as soon as possible, we may lose this Fortress to the spiders."

Adrian saluted and brought out a large box from under one of the metal tables. From the box, he took out a strange-looking rifle that had little redstone lines embedded in it at various places. After that, he took out two regular magazines that had the same little redstone lines embedded in them as the rifle.

"Would you like me to give you a demonstration?" asked Adrian.

Flerra nodded.

Adrian picked up the gun and started to explain. "So, this gun mostly works like a regular assault rifle. That means there's the same button to detach and attack the magazine underneath the stock, and the trigger works the same. Now, the different thing is that this rifle can switch between modes. One is a short burst mode, and one is a long, five-second beam mode. A magazine can fire about ten short laser bursts at a time, although obviously the bursts will be shorter and weaker. There is also a special attachment that lets you aim better with laser sights. We call it the scope. Also, be careful with the recoil - it's insane."

Adrian paused as if looking around for something.

"Lex, where is the prototype scope?" asked Adrian, looking towards another engineer.

"Uh- uh- we- uh- the prototype exploded," stammered Lex, his face turning red.

Adrian closed his eyes in frustration.

"It's fine, Adrian. You have done well. Talk to my assistant for your bonus," smiled Flerra.

CHAPTER ELEVEN

BETRAYAL

The super soldiers and Commander Josh were making the final preparations for their expedition in the teens' cabin.

"Yo, Josh, you got the laser rifle thingy?" said Ron.

"Yes."

"Got the magazines?"

"Yes."

"Got the-"

"For the last time, I have everything, Ron!"

"Geez, okay."

The squad left the supers' cabin and went over to Captain Flerra's cabin to announce their departure.

"Please be safe, guys," said Captain Flerra.

"We'll wipe the floor with Arachnid's butt!" cheered Ron, pumping his fist.

Captain Flerra smiled and the squad left her alone in her cabin. As they walked out of the cabin, they found many endermen and citizens of the Iron Fortress waiting outside. The crowd made a path for them, and the squad waved to the people as they passed. Some people asked them what was going on, and Josh replied that it was a top-secret mission. He didn't want rumours to start, and spies to alert Herobrine and the Spider Queen about their plan.

Alas, it was too late anyway. As the four were ten blocks away from the North Gate, an arrow flew towards Commander Josh.

Neel, with his strong instincts of a ninja and super soldier combined, sensed the arrow. "Commander!"

Commander Josh was too slow to react, and as he turned his head towards the direction in which Neel was looking, the arrow pierced Josh's chest.

The tip of the arrow emerged from Josh's back, and Josh fell to his knees, flashing red.

"No!" yelled Neel, his eyes glowing bright blue.

Ron quickly took out a bunch of potions from his inventory and started dumping them over Josh. Neel started vibrating with rage, and in a few seconds, he was moving so fast he was a blur. He dashed from building to building, trying to find the perpetrator. The civilians around the scene ran around, terrified that the next target would be them.

After a moment, Josh stopped flashing red. Ron was afraid that he was dead, but as Adam checked Josh's pulse and told Ron he was merely unconscious, they both heaved Josh's limp body into the shadows.

Meanwhile, Neel was dashing faster and faster. At one point, he was even less than a blur, if you can imagine that. He left burn marks on the ground he ran on and then came the sounds of blades clashing.

Ron expected Neel to come out of a building with the body of the attacker, but he got the surprise of his life when he saw Neel's limp body flying out and crashing through the wall of another building.

When he saw who the attacker was, Ron was shocked to his core. The enemy was a muscular, bald, dark-skinned human who wore an eyepatch on his left eye. Dayne, their close friend, the blacksmith.

"D- D- Dayne? What's going on?" asked Ron, already knowing the answer.

"You're next, Ron!" grinned Dayne, charging at Ron, his obsidian blade drawn.

Ron was too surprised to react. His life flashed before his eyes. His parents, his childhood, and his good times with Neel in their hometown. His school, the days before the great war. He and his dad playing catch. He knew death was coming.

As Dayne reached within striking range, he raised his obsidian blade. Adam tried to raise his longsword in time to defend Ron, but he was too slow.

Ron closed his eyes, waiting for the blow that would never come. Ron waited for a couple of seconds until he heard Dayne spluttering in pain. He opened his eyes and saw the tip of a glowing purple blade emerging from Dayne's broad chest.

"I'm sorry it had to come to this, Dayne. But, your time in this world is over," said a deep voice.

The sword twisted a sharp ninety degrees, and Dayne choked with pain. The blade twisted again, and

Dayne's eyelids fluttered, and his bleeding body fell to the ground.

The owner of the sword was none other than Scintherus. His face was grim and sad, as Dayne was also a close friend of his. He walked over to Neel and checked his pulse.

"He'll live," he declared.

CHAPTER TWELVE

DEATH TO THE SPIDERS

As Captain Flerra came to know of Dayne's treacherous attempt at Commander Josh's murder, she was deeply grieved.

To be fair, almost everyone in the Fortress was sad. Dayne had been a kind person to everyone, and no one had expected him to be one of the spies and a traitor.

But, as depressing as the situation was, the mission to destroy Arachnid could not be delayed any further than what was necessary. It was decided that General Webley would accompany Ron and Adam in place of Commander Josh, and the last Ender Knight, the corrupted leader, told Captain Flerra that he wished to join the supers in their quest. Ron was now in charge of the laser rifle, and Flerra also gave General Webley a large container of explosives. Flerra told Webley to keep the explosives as a last resort, in case the laser rifle was not enough to destroy the Spider

Queen. Webley grudgingly put the heavy container in his inventory and groaned because of the weight.

"This is going to slow me down a lot, Flerra. But, I will accept your advice," said the Ender General.

The new squad decided to set out at night time, just after sunset. Flerra did not want another hurdle to appear in their path and decided this would be the best course of action.

Neel and Josh would rest in the infirmary. Neel was severely exhausted, and the nurse said that a day of rest would bring him back to full power. Josh was required to stay in bed for a few weeks, as the arrow had pierced Josh's spine and almost broke it in half.

The Ender Knight told the other three that his name was Sirius, and his dragon was Blairion.

The four boarded Blairion, and the pitch-black dragon set off into the night to the north.

The four flew in silence, the memory of Dayne still fresh in their minds. Nobody said a word for almost an hour until Sirius broke the silence.

"I see Mount Silencio up ahead. Is that what we are looking for?" asked Sirius.

"Yes. Let's stop just in front of the mountain. From what I remember, there should be an entrance to the inside of the mountain on the south side," pointed Webley.

As Webley had predicted, there was indeed an opening on the south side. Blairion landed outside and bent down to let the squad get off of him.

"Blairion, boy, you must stay here and await our return," ordered Sirius.

Blairion whined a little but heeded his master's words. He stood guard patiently outside the entrance as the squad departed into the mountain.

The staircase was narrow, and two people could barely stand together side by side.

"I assume Arachnid probably has another exit for herself," said Sirius.

"Yes. But, the last time we attacked the spiders, I remember most of that exit was destroyed. She probably rebuilt it by now with the help of her underling, though," replied Webley.

The four walked down the stairs in silence after that. Ron was lost in his thoughts about Neel and did not realise when the other three stopped.

"Ron!" hissed Adam.

Ron looked around and saw that he almost entered a large chamber in which a few spider soldiers were stationed.

"Sorry!" said Ron.

"It's alright. Can you snipe those spiders in there?" asked Webley.

Ron nodded and took out his mysterious green sniper rifle. He took aim through the iron sights and took out one of the guards.

What Ron didn't account for, was that the spider he shot was in the centre of the chamber, which alerted pretty much everybody in the chamber.

"INTRUDERS!" yelled one of the spiders in a raspy voice.

But, there were only seven or eight spiders in the chamber, and the two endermen disposed of them before Adam and Ron could even react.

"Good going, guys," praised Adam.

Scintherus nodded and Sirius smiled distantly, as if remembering the glories of his past. Adam noticed this and felt bad as he knew that Sirius did not have much time left.

The spiders had dropped some decent loot such as diamonds and iron, but the four did not stop to pick up any of the remnants.

"How much farther is the Queen's chamber?" asked Sirius.

In response, Adam raised his finger to his lips and pressed his ear on the wall.

While Adam was listening for whatever he heard, two spider guards head to toe in Hdiamond spider armour, which somehow was a thing now. The spiders had four swords each, and they lunged towards the squad.

The enders teleported behind the spider soldiers and slashed at their exposed abdomens. One of the spiders poofed while the other screeched in pain.

Ron shot the remaining spider in the head at point-blank range, blowing spider brains everywhere.

"Seriously, Ron?" groaned Webley.

Sirius wiped the spider goo off his armour in disgust. Ron grinned and shrugged, and wiped off the gunk from the muzzle of his gun.

"Guys, Arachnid is behind this wall," whispered Adam.

Everyone tensed up and knew that the fight was about to begin. Webley and Sirius prepared to break the wall down, while Ron switched up his acidic green sniper for the prototype laser rifle, and Adam readied his sword in front of him.

"CHARGE!" yelled Webley.

The endermen rammed straight through the wall, the super soldiers in pursuit. While the Ender General and Sirius were in combat with several spider soldiers, Adam defended Ron from several spiders as he took aim at the massive face of the Spider Queen.

"How long do you need, man?!" yelled Adam, skewering three spiders in a shish kebab.

A blazing hot red beam of light erupted from the head of his rifle and melted straight through one of Arachnid's eyes. Arachnid shrieked with pain, realising how powerful this strange new weapon was. Ron fired a second laser, which Arachnid evaded with ease.

"Damn it!" yelled Ron, charging up the gun again.

"Ron, you've only got one more laser left! Make this count!" yelled Webley, teleporting behind Arachnid and slashing at one of her hairy legs.

Ron frantically turned the reload switch and took aim, at the same time dodging a rogue spider whom Adam missed.

Sirius and Webley were outnumbered. They were taking down spider soldiers by the dozens, but for each spider they poofed, three replaced it. It was clear this battle was not theirs to be won. Webley took a bite to the back, and he instantly poofed the spider behind him with a spinning backslash. But, as he was distracted, Arachnid took the opportunity and whacked him into one of the walls of the massive cavern.

The spiders started rushing towards the fallen enderman, intent on finishing him off.

"No!" yelled Sirius, teleporting in front of Webley to defend him.

In the meantime, Ron had charged up the gun and fired the third and last laser. A spider rammed into Ron as he fired the laser, and the bright beam of heat missed Arachnid's head by a centimetre, singing the hair in that area.

"Well, guys, I guess we're screwed now," Ron grimaced, exchanging the now useless laser rifle for his trusty old magical sniper.

He morphed his sniper into an assault rifle and rained acidic metal on the assailants.

"What are we gonna do now?" shouted Adam, suffering a bite from one of the spiders.

"*There is only one thing we can do,*" said Sirius, *grimly.*

Webley was beginning to come back to consciousness. He eased himself up, twisting his joints to make sure nothing was broken.

"*Webley, hand over the explosives,*" ordered Sirius, as *he poofed two spiders in one skilled slash.*

Webley looked uncertain. "*What are you going to do with them?*"

"*No time to explain. You shall understand once you get out of this,*" said Sirius.

"*You mean we. We will get out of this,*" replied *Webley.*

"*Sure. Now hand over the explosives!*" yelled Sirius.

Webley retrieved the crate of bombs from his inventory and handed the box over to Sirius with a questioning look.

"Now get out of here, you three! I'll come for you!" commanded Sirius.

Ron and Adam did as they were told and sped out of the cavern, leaving the spiders that were swarming them to add themselves to the swarm attacking the enders.

"What are you doing, Sirius?" asked Webley, raising an eyebrow as Sirius yelled at him again to leave.

After another heated exchange, Webley reluctantly agreed to exit the cavern after Sirius promised to rejoin them afterwards.

As Webley teleported outside, he rendezvoused with the super soldiers and Blairion and awaited Sirius.

Suddenly, everyone was blown back.

81

CHAPTER THIRTEEN

RECOVERY

Everyone was blown several blocks away in different directions. Ron flew head-first into a tree and was knocked unconscious. Adam was blown into a clearing, and he got up just to meet a large rock to the head.

General Webley teleported just as the explosion occurred, and rushed to find Ron and Adam. He found Ron in a crumpled heap underneath a nearby tree and slung the boy's body over his shoulder. He teleported from tree to tree, clearing to clearing, trying to find any sign of Adam.

A few minutes later, he spotted Adam's feet jutting out of a pile of rubble.

Panicking, he dropped Ron's body harshly on the ground and teleported to the rubble.

He quickly removed enough of the rocks to free Adam and carefully pulled him out of the rubble.

He breathed a sigh of relief as he checked Adam's pulse. The three were alive, barely. What had happened to Sirius?

Webley did not want to believe it, but he knew that Sirius was dead. He sacrificed himself for the integrity of the mission. Well, he was dying anyway, but this was not how he should have gone out.

"I was tasked with protecting him. He may have been dying, but he had more fight left in him then I ever will. I've failed the leader of the Ender Knights," Webley thought, sadly.

Webley made a small wooden shack for the three of them in a clearing and set down the teenagers on two poorly crafted splintery wooden beds. There was no cushion on any of them, but it would have to do for the time being.

It was not until Webley had built a smoker and furnace did he realised Blairion, Sirius' dragon was missing. Webley had forgotten about the dragon when he was busy tending to the super soldiers.

He left the meat unattended at the smoker and dropped the rest on the floor as he teleported outside.

It was not nighttime yet, but Webley only had about thirty minutes until the mobs would begin to spawn.

He teleported from clearing to clearing and checked any large space where a dragon could be. At last, when he was almost blown up by a rogue creeper, he caught sight of a pitch-black lump of a tail.

The tail emerged from a massive pile of rocks.

"How in the Nether did I miss that?" said Webley, shaking his head.

After he almost got bitten on his leg by an escaped spider, Webley realised he needed to act fast if he wanted to get Blairion out of the debris before some mob got a lucky hit on him.

He hastily teleported rock after rock, even a few random tree trunks off of Blairion, all the while pausing to deal with some nighttime mobs.

Soon, he was able to free the unconscious dragon and then wondered what in the Nether he was going to do with him. He couldn't just very well leave the poor creature out to fend for himself, the zombies would eat him alive. Instead, Webley chose to build a small shelter around Blairion out of dirt. It took about an hour or so, and he was exhausted by the end of it. He decided to call it a day after he lit up the interior with a couple of torches. As soon as he teleported to the small shack of the super soldiers and went inside, he collapsed from exhaustion as soon as he closed the door.

CHAPTER FOURTEEN

NIGHTMARES

Neel was running from the pillagers. Arrows pierced all throughout his body. Nasty visions of his parents' corpses filled his mind.

He weaved through the dead bodies of his friends, and Ron's sickening cries as he was blown to bits by the shotgun still echoed in his head...

He hid in the houses of his town, each one being blown to pieces by TNT.

He came across his house and found the corpses of his parents once more lying on the ground, blood splattered everywhere.

As Neel heard the footsteps of a pillager coming up behind him, he was obliged to turn around. But, this was not a pillager, this was the maniacal Herobrine himself.

Herobrine laughed and raised his glowing white sword. Blood dripped off the sword, the remains of so many victims of the evil glitch.

Herobrine suddenly stopped laughing and swung his blade downwards.

Neel woke up in a cold sweat.

"Mom! Dad!" yelled Neel, panicking.

"Calm down! You are in a safe place," said a feminine voice.

Neel turned to see a dark-skinned woman in a doctor's uniform looking down at him in a gentle manner. Mary, the fortress' head doctor.

"Where are my parents? Are they alright? Are they dead?" asked Neel, panicking once more.

"Yes, they are safe. Probably. I don't know!" replied Mary.

Neel realised he was being irrational. Why would Mary know anything about his parents? But, they were probably safe. He had seen them leave the town in one piece with his own eyes.

All the same, he was concerned about their fate. He had escaped with his friends to Fort Torro, and had back then hoped that they would be in Fort Linux. Once the two forts united as the Iron Fortress, Neel's parents were not there either.

The only thing remaining was that they were either dead or captured by Herobrine's forces. Or, there was another safehouse somewhere out in the overworld.

Neel decided that there were more pressing matters to deal with at the moment. He would find his parents later, once the End was freed from the Wither Kingdom.

Neel looked at his surroundings. Of course, he was in the underground hospital of the bunker. He was in the special patients room and Josh lay beside him on another bed, his entire torso covered in bandages.

"Is he alright? He doesn't look too good..." said Neel, concerned about the commander.

"He will need to rest for a few months at the least. The arrow that pierced his chest had a tip made of vamiscite, the most deadly and purest form of vamberite. Even boiled water mixed with a healing potion and a regeneration potion could not heal him fully, it only released him from his constant pain and stopped the bleeding," replied Mary. "He won't be on the battlefield for a long time, I'm afraid."

Neel thanked Mary for the information and asked her if he was fit to leave the hospital. Mary permitted him to leave on condition of not over-exerting himself and returning every week for two months for a check-up.

Neel agreed and rushed out of the room. Mary shook her head and went to tend to Josh's medication.

The first thing Neel did after getting out of the hospital was try to find his friends. But, to his surprise, they were nowhere to be found. He went to their apartment, he visited Dayne's old workshop, which stinged with betrayal. Shaking his head and teary-eyed, he left the workshop, the memories of the last six months reappearing in his head. It was painful, as Dayne had been one of his best friends after he came to Fort Torro. All the same, he had to move on. He had to focus on the war. He visited all the places Adam and Ron liked to go to, but could not find them anywhere.

At a loss, he decided to visit Captain Flerra. She would know where they went. So, he rushed out of his apartment and ran over to Flerra's cabin. He was surprised to see that Tom, the security guard who always stood by the door, was not present. Neel shrugged and knocked on the door.

After a few minutes of silence, he knocked again. And again. And again. And-

"Have you gone bloody mad, mate?" said a rough voice. "The Captain and Tom ain't here till Sunday. Stop makin' such a bloody racket, I'm tryna get a bit of sleep over here."

Neel turned around to see a muscular, light-skinned man in boxer shorts and a white vest.

"Why in the Nether do you want to see her anyway? It's bloody two o'clock in the morning!" exclaimed the man.

Neel looked up at the sky. It was, indeed, very dark. Neel had not noticed how late it had become while he was searching for his friends.

"I'm Neel, one of the super soldiers. I urgently needed to see Captain Flerra, but I guess I can't do that now. Also, my bad bro, I didn't realise it was so late," Neel saluted and left the guy shaking his head in annoyance.

CHAPTER FIFTEEN

ANOTHER ENEMY?

"Hey, General! Get up, bro! It's one in the afternoon, sleepyhead!" yelled a voice.

Webley woke up to getting kicked lightly in the butt. He turned around to see Ron, grinning wildly with a smoking steak in his hand.

"General Webley is awake?" said Adam, looking up from the piece of meat he was cooking in the smoker.

"Indeed, I am. When did you guys wake up?" asked Webley, stretching his long, dark limbs.

"Eh, I don't know. A few hours ago? You didn't exactly leave us in a comfortable position to sleep in, you

know," said Ron, taking a large bite of his steak. "Mm, this stuff is good!"

"Heh, sorry about that. I had to make sure Blairion was safe. Can I get a cooked pork chop?" said Webley.

"Coming right up," said Adam, throwing another piece of meat into the smoker.

After a short pause, Webley asked about any signs of Sirius.

"Uh, um, I don't think he made it out alive. I'm sorry, Webley," said Adam, sadly.

Webley was crestfallen. He was supposed to be in charge of the mission, and make sure everyone made it out alive.

"I failed the mission," said Webley, miserably.

"No, you didn't. The mission was to destroy the Spider Queen, and I'll even bet my sniper that she was vaporised in that blast. I know it's sad we lost Sirius, but he knew his fate was sealed even if he survived the mission, and so he sacrificed himself to guarantee our survival. In the end, he died a hero, and that's what matters," said Adam, putting a hand on Webley's thin, dark shoulder.

"Thank you, Adam, I appreciate it," said Webley, forcing a smile.

"I hate to ruin this touching moment, but what are we gonna do now?" said Ron. "Sirius is dead but we aren't, so let's go back home."

"Ron! What's wrong with you?!" yelled Adam.

"What? I'm just stating facts. He's six blocks under, and whining about it isn't gonna bring him back," said Ron, shrugging.

Adam facepalmed and was about to retaliate to Ron's insensitivity to the situation when Webley raised his hand for Adam to stop.

"It's fine. Ron, if anything, we should respect Sirius' death. But, you're right, sitting here and being sad about it is not what Sirius would have wanted. We have a war to return to," said Webley, determined.

After everyone was fed and Blairion was tended to, the group started packing up the shelter. Adam put away his smoker and removed the furniture, meanwhile, Ron and Webley tore down the walls and roof. Building materials were always welcomed in their inventories.

They climbed aboard Blairion, and flew up far into the sky, beginning the journey back towards the Iron Fortress.

After a few minutes, Ron narrowed his eyes, and Webley noticed this.

"What are you looking at?" said Webley.

"What do you mean what am I looking at? You guys don't see that massive building in the distance, to the left of us?" said Ron, baffled. "Did you go blind after *the explosion?"*

"Shut up. I don't see anything except for endless plains as far as I can see. What are you talking about? You must have hit your head too hard after the explosion," retorted Webley.

"Both of y'all, be quiet. General, you should have some sort of maturity above Ron. He doesn't know any better," said Adam.

"Hey!" frowned Ron.

"And, to answer your question, Ron, no, I do not see a random massive building to the left of us," continued Adam, without pause.

"Well, I know I'm not going insane. Blairion, you see that building right? Well, change the direction and go towards it!" said Ron, almost yelling.

In response, Blairion abruptly turned left, almost throwing Adam off its back.

"*Hey, hey, calm down!*" *yelled Adam.*

If Blairion heard Adam, he did not appear to heed his words. For some reason, upon Ron's command, he started flying a lot faster towards the supposed building in the distance.

"*What's wrong, Blairion? Holy nether, what is that?*" *gasped Webley, pointing towards the massive structure that Ron had noticed earlier.*

"*So, now you blind guys see it. What do you think it is?*" *asked Ron, scratching his blocky head with one arm, his other hand holding onto the scales of the dragon.*

The plains stretched out for hundreds of blocks in front of their path, with dense oak forests on either side of the plains. The occasional cave jutted out from the flat grounds, giving it some variation. The plains ended abruptly at the massive structure, and the two oak forests met behind the strange building.

The building itself was a central massive skyscraper, with smaller buildings and structures surrounding it for about a couple hundred blocks on each side. Surrounding the entire compound hexagonally was an incredibly thick wall, probably dozens of blocks thick, easily several times thicker than the walls of the Iron Fortress. On top of all of this, the outer layers of the walls appeared to be made of obsidian, which made the wall virtually impenetrable.

"What... in... Minecraftia... IS THAT?" exclaimed Ron, almost scaring Adam off Blairion's back for the second time.

"You don't think that's an enemy of ours, do you, Webley? If it is, it's not far from the Iron Fortress, and we don't stand a chance against something like that. If the structure itself is so awe-inspiring, you can only imagine how powerful their army would be," said Adam, nervous at the prospect of such an opponent.

"We don't have any known allies, Adam. I have little doubt that it is an enemy base. Now, let's scout it and see what's going on, and we will report to Warmaster Scintherus and Captain Flerra about the situation," said Webley, melancholically.

Originally, Webley intended for the squad to stealthily observe the scenario in the base, but that plan was scrapped when Blairion blew their cover by letting out a terrifying roar when they were in a three-hundred-block radius of the unknown fortress.

"Well, so much for sneakiness," snorted Ron. "What are we going to do now, turn back?"

Webley turned around, and his mouth fell open. "I don't believe that's an option anymore."

CHAPTER SIXTEEN

SPARRING

Neel had come to find out from a guard on the wall that Ron, Adam, Sirius and General Webley had gone on a mission to destroy the spider base. Sirius had substituted Neel, and General Webley had substituted Commander Josh. Neel was not angry that he did not get to go on the mission as he knew that the mission was urgent and its success was of utmost importance.

After some thought, Neel decided that he would put his time into training to get to level fifty and get ahead of Adam, and would afterwards devote himself to finding the whereabouts of his parents. He was starting to miss them, and he hoped they were still alive.

So, after he had enquired with the guard, he headed over to the training area of the elite soldiers, where another commander called Commander Thomas was tasked with training the soldiers. He arrived at the training grounds and found Thomas sparring with another soldier.

Neel had never really trained inside the training grounds of the Iron Fortress, as after the completion of the behemoth project, they had been involved in battles and events and never really got to visit the grounds. It wasn't spectacular, just similar to the one at Fort Torro. It was a large, fenced area with several dummies and weights, and there was a large shed at the far left corner, which was probably used for storing wooden or stone weapons and armour of different types.

Commander Thomas was using a double-sided wooden katana, and his movements were extremely fast and agile as he ducked and weaved through his opponent. Neel never saw him get hit even once, but he was stabbing and slashing his opponent repeatedly and elegantly, making it look like a walk in the park. The soldier flashed red quite a lot of times, and just as Thomas was about to land a downward slash that looked like it would have hurt a lot, the soldier held up his hand.

"Stop! I'm at four and a half hearts! I need some food," said the soldier, getting up.

The Commander gave him a copper ingot and told the soldier to go get himself a beetroot and potato salad from the grocery store.

"But sir, I wanted a bu-"

"No buts, Carter. If you want to get stronger, you have to stick to a diet," ordered Thomas, sternly.

The soldier sulked away down a corner, and Neel approached Thomas.

"Good morning, Neel. Looking for some sparring?" said Thomas, giving a polite grin.

"Sir, I am. Can I spar with one of your soldiers?" asked Neel.

"One of my soldiers? No can't do, buddy," said Thomas, laughing at the annoyed look on Neel's face. "Just kidding, you can spar with me!"

Neel knew Thomas wouldn't say no. He was a gruff, muscular, light-skinned, middle-aged guy who looked like he was probably mean or rude, but he was a kind-hearted dude who was practically the opposite of his stereotype.

Thomas told him to go retrieve wooden replicas of his dual blades, which Neel learnt were called wakizashi, and were not typically used to dual wield. They were from an unknown background but were suspected to originate from a race of ninjas that had been wiped out by the Vamblin Ninjas.

Neel came out of the wooden shed, a wooden wakizashi in each of his hands.

Commander Thomas was flaunting his double-sided katana with a wild grin on his face. "Are you ready to get destroyed?"

"You'll be the one getting destroyed today, Commander," said Neel, getting into an attack position.

Without waiting for a response, Neel jumped into the air and landed beside the Commander so swiftly that Thomas was almost taken off-guard. Neel swiped at Thomas with both of his wakizashi, but Thomas easily parried every single stroke, and Neel was getting frustrated. He decided to try out a move he never thought of executing before. He swung his sword as if to strike Thomas from the left, but just as Thomas was preparing to parry the blade, Neel stopped mid-swing and ducked, and then stabbed Thomas with the tip of his sword.

"Ow! I'll get you back for that, you cheeky rascal!" yelled Thomas, holding his stomach, where the stab of Neel's sword had brought out a bit of blood.

Neel grinned, having landed his first hit on the Commander. He thought this was going to be easy from then on, but he had no idea that Thomas had just been holding back. Neel realised what a predicament he had gotten himself into when Thomas' movements suddenly became quicker and harder to parry. Thomas swung both sides of his double-sided katana in rapid succession down on Neel's head, Neel only managed to parry one of the sides and the other one struck his shoulder.

"How... are... you... so... fast?" gasped Neel, barely able to get the words out.

"I may not have the powers you super soldiers have, but I have superior experience and skill," replied Thomas, now landing blow after blow on poor Neel.

Neel was now too exhausted to use his super speed and agility, and his movements were incredibly sluggish. Thomas was still going strong and if he was getting even a little bit tired, he was displaying no signs of it.

"Stop! Stop! I'm at two hearts!" yelled Neel, dashing out of the way of Thomas' strike with his last bit of energy.

Thomas' katana embedded itself in the dirt.

"Why did you wait so long to announce your low health? I could have killed you!" scolded Thomas.

"I'm sorry! I didn't realise that I was so low on hearts," replied Neel, hastily. "Can I go get some food now, if you don't mind?"

"Potato and beetroot salad," Thomas reminded him.

Neel knew better than to argue with him. Instead, he dropped his wakizashi on the grass and went in the direction of the grocery store with a frown on his face.

CHAPTER SEVENTEEN

HUSKS AND SAND DRAGONS

Ron and Adam followed Webley's gaze and were astonished to see what was following them.

It looked like Blairion, but instead of pitch-black skin, it had sandy, cream-coloured scales covering its body, and had white eyes instead of purple eyes.

It had a diamond-clad husk riding it, who wielded a netherite sword.

Blairion, seeing as there was only one dragon, decided to make a run for it as he turned right, but his eyes went wide as he realised two more sandy dragons had flanked him from either side.

"Intruder! Land outside the walls or we will blow you out of the sky! I repeat, land outside the walls or we will not hesitate to destroy you, corrupted knights!" yelled the husk behind them.

"Corrupted knights? What does he mean? Blairion, heed the husk's command!" ordered General Webley, tapping on Blairion's dark scales to make sure he got the message.

Almost instantly after Webley's communication, Blairion dived down, making to land on the grass just outside the fortified entrance of the unknown compound.

Blairion ceased to a halt and Webley, Adam and Ron got off his back. A second later, the other three dragons landed and their riders jumped off as well.

"State your business here, corrupted knight, and companions," ordered the middle husk, who appeared to be the leader of the group, in a raspy voice.

"We are not corrupted Ender Knights. I am General Webley, second in command after Warmaster Scintherus. These are two super soldiers, Ron and

Adam. Who are you, and what is this structure?" said Webley, suspiciously.

"I doubt you are who you claim to be," the husk narrowed his eyes. "Neutralise them."

The husks exchanged their swords for crossbows faster than Webley could react and fired some sort of darts at the General and the super soldiers. Webley felt the tip of the dart pierce his neck, and started to feel the strange liquid in the darts seep into his dark skin.

"What in the Nether? What have you freaks done to us?" whispered Ron, feeling suddenly exhausted as the liquid in the dart carried out its effect.

Ron fell to the ground, seemingly unconscious. Adam tried to support himself on his longsword but ended up falling to the ground as well, the sword still embedded in the dirt. Webley tried to teleport but was unable to due to the lack of energy. He reached into his inventory for his energy blade, but his exhaustion got the better of him and he fell to the ground before he could touch the inventory slot the blade was in.

"Hendrick, since when did corrupted Ender Knights have humans for companions?" asked one of the husks, unsure of his actions.

"Who are you to question my decisions?" sneered Hendrick. "Utter another word and I'll have you on a charge."

The other husk scowled at Hendrick but held his tongue as he knew he would face consequences if he talked back to his superior.

"Now quit frowning at me and pick these idiots up from the ground. We'll ask Lord Hazard what to do with them," ordered Hendrick.

The scowling husk opened his mouth to insult Hendrick, but the third husk put his hand on his shoulder.

"It's not worth it, Hayden," he whispered.

Haydor clenched and unclenched his fists under the harsh gaze of Hendrick.

"Yes, sir," sighed Hayden, tucking away his netherite sword to pick up the unconscious body of General Webley.

Hendrick gestured for the third husk to pick up Ron, while he picked up Adam.

"This one's heavy. Must be a tank," remarked Hendrick, barely concealing the strain on his arms in front of his soldiers.

Once the three unconscious bodies were carefully placed atop the backs of the sand dragons, the husks flew off towards the building.

CHAPTER EIGHTEEN

THE HUSKAN EMPIRE

Ron awoke with a startle on the cold sandstone floor.

"I thought this stuff was supposed to be hot," he said, rubbing his neck where the neutralising dart had struck a few hours before. "Where am I?"

He looked around the small room. The walls were made out of reinforced sandstone, with obsidian streaks running through the stone.

"I've never seen anything like this," marvelled Ron, running his fingers through the even colder obsidian

branches.

"It's a marvel of engineering, isn't it, corrupted knight?" said a deep voice, from a sand-coloured tinted glass window on one side of the room, that Ron hadn't noticed before.

"Who are you?" growled Ron, turning towards the camouflaged window and taking out his acidic sniper rifle.

"How do you still have that? I stripped you of all your belongings," exclaimed the voice. "What is this sorcery?"

"Guess you didn't check hard enough," shrugged Ron, aiming at the window.

There were muffled sounds from the window as if the person behind it were straining to duck. All of a sudden, two diamond-clad husks emerged from a concealed sand-coloured iron door.

"What's next, a sand-coloured minigun camera?" grumbled Ron, morphing his sniper into an assault *rifle, much to the shock and horror of the two husks.*

"Who are you? What kind of enderman can change the form of his weapon?" said one of the husks, in a frightened voice.

"Are you serious? I look like an enderman to you?" exclaimed Ron, bewildered at the remark.

"Okay, yeah, you aren't pitch black," nodded the husk, his blade still raised. "But, then why were you an accomplice of the corrupted Ender Knight? Aren't humans supposed to be against Herobrine?"

"He's not a corrupted Ender Knight! He is General Webley, the top most general of the endermen. I am a super soldier. Why would you be against corrupted Ender Knights anyway, husk? Aren't the husks allied with Herobrine like the zombies?" asked Ron, raising his finger to the trigger.

"Allied to Herobrine? We are nothing like those pathetic zombies. Do not dare to insult us like that. Lord Hazard has been against Herobrine since the very beginning of the Great War," spat the husk, his sandy eyebrows creasing in anger.

"Fine, bro, I'm sorry. If you guys are really against Herobrine, you would know that I, as a super soldier,

am very important to this war," said Ron, lowering his sniper.

"Well, looks like you're very full of yourself," said the husk, much to Ron's indignation. "It is not my place to conclude whether you're an asset or a liability. Though, you're probably the latter. I will let that decision rest with Lord Hazard."

Ron's mouth fell open at the insult. "Why, you little-"

"Keep your mouth shut, human," said the husk who had kept quiet until now. "We will now take you to your companions, and request an audience with Lord Hazard."

Ron chose not to open his mouth and followed the satisfied husks out of the cell. They emerged in a long reinforced sandstone corridor, three blocks wide and three blocks tall, with jail cells on either side. He saw several different monsters in the cells, ranging from wither skeletons to spiders.

"Are all of these prisoners of war?" asked Ron, looking at a specifically large mutant zombie.

"Yes. The Huskan Army has captured many different forts and outposts near this base. We have also extended our reach to the Nether, where we assist the Piglins in their battles with the zombie pigmen," replied one of the husks.

"Why don't you go ahead and tell him about Lord Hazard's secret project as well, Hock," said the other husk, sarcastically.

Ron didn't even know that undead could blush, but Hock reddened in embarrassment and coughed to hide it.

"Hey, why don't you husks stink like zombies? Aren't you guys undead too?" asked Ron, suddenly remembering the stark smell of zombies after the group passed a particularly smelly one.

"Like I said, apart from being undead, we are nothing like our zombie counterparts," sighed Hock, not wanting to be compared to a zombie.

Before Ron could respond, the three had arrived at an iron door guarded by another two diamond-clad husks. The guards opened the iron door, and the three passed through it in a single file line with Ron in the middle.

On the other side of the heavy iron door, they were greeted by 4 other diamond-clad husks escorting General Webley and Adam.

"Hey, wait a minute, where's our dragon?" asked Ron.

"What, you wanted him to turn up in this room too?" asked one of the husks sarcastically. "He's in the damned dragon stables. Now shut up, before I make you."

Ron looked towards the husk's side where the husk's hand rested on his netherite blade. Ron nodded, to the husk's satisfaction, and the husk removed his hand from his sword. Adam was kicking the ground in front of him, and Webley was surveying the room as if looking for a means to escape. It was a six-by-six room, just enough for a holding of the present size. It seemed like a waiting room, and there was another iron door just across the first one.

Suddenly, a husk in full enchanted netherite armour opened the door. "Lord Hazard will see you now."

The diamond-clad husks escorted the three through the door, into a massive reinforced sandstone and gilded blackstone chamber. In the centre of the chamber was a massive gilded blackstone throne atop which an unarmoured husk with glowing yellow eyes sat with one leg crossed above the other.

"Welcome! I am Hazard, emperor of the husks. What brings you to our humble abode?" smiled the strange husk, spreading his arms.

"Why are your eyes yellow? Are you a cousin of Herobrine?" blurted Ron.

Two netherite-clad husks immediately took out their glistening dark blades and angrily started towards Ron. But, Hazard took it in good stride and laughed heartily, and motioned for his guards to stand down. The guards nodded in unison, tucked their blades back into their scabbards and stood at attention.

"*You are lucky I am not so easily offended as Herobrine. No, I am not related to Herobrine,*" replied Hazard, refusing to elaborate further.

"*That's cool and all, but then why are your eyes glowing yellow?*" pressed Ron, determined to get an answer.

"*That is a story for another time. Now, you will answer my question. Why have you come here? Your captain and the endermen know nothing of our presence in this location,*" said Hazard, staring unblinkingly at Ron.

General Webley intercepted Ron just as he was about to speak. "*We stumbled upon this location while we were returning from massacring the spiders.*"

"*You three are the ones responsible for the destruction of the spiders? Impossible. The base was blown from inside out,*" Hazard narrowed his eyes at Webley.

"*Our fourth companion, the previous leader of the Ender Knights sacrificed himself to save the rest of us,*" replied Webley, recalling the upsetting memory.

"*A noble sacrifice, then. Very well, I need not further question you all, for I think you are telling the truth.*

One last matter to deal with. It has come to my attention that the End dimension has fallen to the Wither Skeletons. As a sign of our alliance with Captain Flerra and Warmaster Scintherus, and a token of apology for our absence in the war for so long, you will take the Second Elite Legion and these escorts with you," ordered Hazard. "You are dismissed."

Before Webley could open his mouth to speak, the six escort husks roughly shoved them back towards the door they came from.

"The emperor does not require an audience with you anymore. Keep your mouth shut and keep moving," ordered one of the husks.

The three were taken back to the middle room, and instead of going through the opposite iron door that led back to the jail cells, they walked through yet another concealed exit. They emerged in an armoury, where General Webley and Adam's weapons were returned to them. Somehow, Ron's weapon was never discovered in his inventory in the first place. A mystery, for sure, but no one knew the answer as to why. The armoury was a massive chamber, probably a hundred blocks tall and easily twice the size of Lord Hazard's private chamber. It was a twenty by-twenty room with several sections filled to the brim with armour and weapons of various types and materials. There were ten different balcony style floors that wrapped around the sides and corners of the room, and in the centre was a five-by-five skylight. In the five-by-five skylight area there was a strange contraption that contained a missile similar to the ones used in trebuchets; long, sharply pointed, somewhat like a giant bullet, except this one was twice as large.

"What's that?" Ron pointed towards the machine.

"It's a missile silo," replied Hock. "I am not allowed to disclose anything else."

"Oh, come on," said Ron. "Where's the fun in that?"

"There's absolutely nothing fun about a missile silo," chuckled another husk. "There's no point in asking us about the silo. We are loyal to our orders."

Ron looked at the silo one last time before they went through another iron door, and were exposed to the insane heat of the dragons' stables. It was a massive outdoor structure, with easily a thousand dragons kept there.

"How- How have you guys kept this hidden for so long?" said Ron, his jaw-dropping as he took in the sheer largeness.

"This is a fairly new base. It's only been about a year since we've finished construction," said a husk. "I've heard that you lot built the Iron Fortress in a span of a few days, so this shouldn't be much of a surprise for you."

"The Iron Fortress is nothing compared to this megastructure," marvelled Ron. "What happened to your old base?"

Hock opened his mouth to speak, but his companion cut him off, glaring at him.

"That is classified," said the husk, his expression one of warning.

Hock swallowed what he was going to say and nodded. As they were passing through the large stables, one of the husks from the group went to talk to a stablemaster. After a few moments of waiting, the husk returned with good news.

"The stablemaster will provide us with the dragons as soon as we need them," grinned the husk. "All we have to do is mobilise the Second Elite Legion, as Lord Hazard said. Let's go to the barracks."

"Why are we going to the barracks?" asked Ron.

"Are you dense? Never mind, let's go," the husk shook his head in despair.

Ron grinned as the group walked towards an intersection in the massive stables. There were four ways to go - the end of the stables, back the way they came, towards another entrance to the armoury, and a huge arch that led to the barracks.

As they entered the huge chamber called the barracks, the group walked over to a large desk where a husk wearing a suit and glasses sat.

"What do you want? I've got other work to do," said the husk, looking over the rim of his glasses.

"We request the service of the Second Elite Legion, as per the order of the emperor," said one of the husks, Horus.

"Second Elite Legion? I'm afraid I can't do that," said the clerk, matter-of-factly. "Do you have a written document signed by the emperor on you?"

"Er, no, I don't. I'm not asking, clerk. I'm telling you to hand over the documents to assign the Second Elite Legion to our mission," snarled Horus. "Now, I'm sure you like all your limbs on your body, don't you?"

The clerk paled. "You wouldn't dare."

Horus cracked his knuckles and slammed his fist on the acacia wood table.

"I won't ask again."

The clerk rummaged through a drawer and violently threw a folder at Horus' face. Horus caught the folder mere inches from his face and sneered.

Horus started walking towards another doorway and beckoned the others to follow. As they emerged through the door, they were greeted by a lavish chamber filled with hundreds of husks milling about.

"Welcome to the Elite Quarters, reserved for the best of the best," scowled Horus. "And the ones who can pay their way into here."

CHAPTER NINETEEN

WAR DISCUSSIONS

"Warmaster Scintherus, the EnderLord has returned," saluted an ender soldier, entering Captain Flerra's cabin.

"We'll be right there," nodded Scintherus.

Scintherus and Flerra got up from their chairs and followed the soldier outside. The EnderLord was surveying the bunker from his massive height and was wearing a strange set of purple armour similar to the Ender Knights. He had a massive enchanted purple sword strapped to his back.

"Hello, Flerra, hello Scintherus. The new Ender Knights have completed their training. Terynn, the elite ender soldier, is the leader of the knights as you requested," smiled the EnderLord.

Scintherus saluted the EnderLord. "Where are they, my lord?"

"I have sent them on their first mission. Their task is to take down a pillager fortress in the southern region of the Savannah," replied the EnderLord. "It's no small task, as the pillager fortress is the second largest in the known world, I believe, with over ten thousand illagers. But, the Ender Knights are strong and Terynn can be relied on to lead them with honour."

"Thank you for helping us in this time of need. We have a decent-sized army now, are we going to take back the End?" said Flerra.

The EnderLord smiled at Scintherus. "The Ender Knights can be expected to return in about a month. The region is very far off, as you probably know. As for taking back the End, that is Scintherus' call. After all, he is the Warmaster of the endermen."

"There is another thing I wanted to discuss. Ron and Adam haven't returned with General Webley yet. I feel this is a matter of concern, so what are we to do?" said Flerra.

"They are in good hands at the moment," replied the EnderLord. "I won't say anything else about this to you, as you will discover it soon."

Flerra stared at the EnderLord for a moment but realised it would do no good. Instead, she decided to press on other matters.

"Speaking of falling into good hands, the zombie pigmen are on the verge of defeat. Our newfound allies, the piglins, have slowly eaten away their supply lines and have gradually taken over their territory. The nether may be experiencing a revolution," suggested Flerra.

"The Nether is not our concern at the moment," the EnderLord said firmly. "We must focus on the Overworld and the End."

Flerra was annoyed at this dismissal, but she knew that the EnderLord was right. There was no point in worrying about the Nether when they had threats to deal with in their home dimensions.

CHAPTER TWENTY

WAR IS COMING

The dragons flew through this sky in massive numbers, like migrating birds. How he missed those birds.

Herobrine looked through his massive glass chamber at the top of his palace, staring at the massive Huskan Elite Legion travelling in the distance.

A netherite-clad super skeleton walked into the chamber and stood to attention.

"Lord Herobrine, the super skeleton battalion has been mobilised, as you asked. What are your commands for them?" bowed the super skeleton.

The skeleton's hoarse voice broke Herobrine's train of thought and Herobrine stared at him for a few moments. The skeleton was used to Herobrine's unnerving behaviour, as he used to be the head of Herobrine's bodyguard, and was now promoted to the rank of General after SlickArrow's betrayal.

Herobrine's expressionless face turned cold. "You have only mobilised one battalion, Zero?"

"Er, yes, my lord, that is what you ordered," replied Zero, confused at his tone.

Herobrine took a deep breath. "That is my fault. One battalion will not suffice to support the wither skeletons to defend the End. Make sure one more super skeleton battalion is mobilised, along with a mutant zombie battalion and sixty zombie divisions."

"Sir, that would leave the palace next to defenceless. The rest of our troops have been sent to the Nether," protested Zero.

Herobrine clenched his fists in frustration. "I forgot about that. Alright, leave the sixty zombie divisions here and call back a few Vamblin Ninja divisions to protect the palace. Make sure the rest have left for the End by dawn."

Zero nodded, bowed once more, and left the glass chamber.

Herobrine turned back towards the window and stared unblinkingly at the massive cloud of dragons in the distance.

Suddenly, he felt he was being watched. A cold sensation of paranoia, a sense of dread that he was vaguely familiar with.

Then came the voice. "You've grown soft, Herobrine."

Epilogue

"Horus! Horus! Get over here!" yelled Hock, as the husk soldiers were setting up camp for the night.

Horus emerged from a leather tent and rolled his eyes as he saw Hock looking into his spyglass.

"What do you see on the horizon now, o'mighty one?" mocked Horus.

Hock did not respond, and just stared into the spyglass, his mouth slightly agape. Horus was intrigued.

"Okay, what have you found this time?" said Horus.

Hock shivered as he handed the spyglass to Horus. "You won't like this."

There were thousands of silhouettes on the horizon, thousands of armed monsters heading straight for the Huskan campsite. Horus shivered as he realised what he and his men were facing.

Suddenly, the column stopped and a voice echoed throughout the desert. "Surrender yourselves, now! I am not known for showing mercy, but as you are undead as well, this time you will be forgiven for your treachery to me. Bow, bow before the Necrolord!"

Horus mumbled something and tried to walk backwards before he tripped. "Take to arms! I repeat, take to arms! We are under attack, take to arms!"